GUS

THE PUPPY PLACE

Don't miss any of these other stories by Ellen Miles!

THE PUPPY PLACE

GUS

ELLEN MILES

SCHOLASTIC INC.

For Brooke, Maddie, and Claire, 4th grade animal protectors.
Their hard work and dedication led to changes in Illinois state
law regulating puppy mills. I'm so proud of them!

ISBN 978-0-545-72646-7

Cover art by Tim O'Brien
Original cover design by Steve Scott

12 11 10 9 8 7 6 5 4 3 2   15 16 17 18 19 20/0

Printed in the U.S.A.   40

First printing, May 2015

CHAPTER ONE

"What are you talking about?" Lizzie glared at Daphne. "Why would we need a different president?"

Daphne shrugged. "Maybe it's just time for a change."

Lizzie did not agree. Why did they need to change anything? Everything was working just fine. She looked around the table at Maria and Brianna. Maria, her best friend, did not look back at her. Brianna was looking at Daphne — *her* best friend. Lizzie threw up her hands. "This wasn't even on our agenda for today," she said.

It was Friday afternoon, time for the weekly meeting of the AAA Dynamic Dog Walkers. As always, they were at the home of Lizzie Peterson, president. She was president for a lot of good reasons. Number one: she had invented the whole idea of a dog-walking business and had lined up the very first clients. Number two: she knew the most about dogs. She had a library full of books about dogs, and an aunt who ran a doggy day care. She volunteered every week at the local animal shelter, Caring Paws. On top of all that, her family fostered puppies. They took care of puppies who needed help until they found them fantastic forever homes. Number three: she had a lot of good ideas. Number four — well, Lizzie couldn't think of number four just then, but only because Daphne had started talking again.

"It's, like, I just think maybe we need a breath of fresh air, some new ideas." Daphne looked at

Brianna while she spoke, and Brianna nodded eagerly.

"Fresh air is great," said Lizzie, crossing her arms. "So are new ideas. But do we really need a different president to have those?" She looked at Maria, waiting for her to nod the way Brianna had nodded at Daphne.

Maria was still looking down at the kitchen table.

"Anyway, we already got some fresh air when we invited you two to join the business," Lizzie went on, looking back at Brianna and Daphne. "Remember?" The business had originally been just Lizzie and Maria, and they'd been doing just fine. They'd had all the clients they could handle. Then Brianna and Daphne started a competing business, Premium Pet Dog Walkers. Lizzie was furious when she found one of their flyers — offering a lower price per walk — in her very own neighborhood!

"Sure, I remember," said Daphne. "But I also remember that you only invited us to join when you started a price war and ended up with more clients than you could handle."

Lizzie sighed. "What's your point?" she asked. She should have known that having Brianna and Daphne join their business was asking for trouble. Daphne was just so bossy, a total know-it-all.

"My point is that Brianna and I have been part of the business for a while now, and I think it's time that somebody else had a chance to be president," Daphne said slowly, as if she were talking to a kindergartner. "What part of that don't you understand?"

Lizzie slid down in her seat and dangled her hand toward the floor to pet Buddy's head. Buddy licked her hand. *Buddy*, Lizzie thought. *My true best friend. The only loyal one in the room.* Buddy had been one of her family's foster dogs — until the Petersons had decided they were his perfect forever family.

Lizzie frowned at her friend. Why wasn't Maria speaking up? Didn't she see that this was just Daphne trying to grab all the power? Daphne always had to have things her way.

Maria cleared her throat. "Maybe . . ." she started off in a very small voice, "maybe it's not such a bad idea to shake things up a little bit."

Lizzie could not believe her ears. Even her best friend was turning against her. "Are you kidding?" she asked.

Maria shrugged. "What if we just agreed to have an election?" she asked. "We could even make it a secret vote."

"Yes!" said Daphne. "That's all I'm asking for. Like, the democratic process."

"That seems fair," Brianna agreed.

Lizzie shook her head slowly. This was ridiculous.

"Fine," she said. She put both hands down on the table and pushed back her chair. "If that's the way you all want it, that's how it will be. We'll take a vote at our next meeting. Now, if you don't mind, we have some dogs to walk." She stood up and stalked out of the room without waiting for the others to follow.

"Lizzie," Maria called after her as they left the house. "Come on, Lizzie, don't be mad."

Lizzie let her friend catch up. It would be silly not to, since they were both headed to the same neighborhood to walk dogs. "I'm not mad," Lizzie said, even though she sort of was. "I'm just . . . surprised, I guess. I thought I was doing a pretty good job as president."

"You were!" said Maria. "You are."

"Then why do we have to change?" Lizzie kicked at a pebble that lay on the sidewalk.

Maria was quiet. "Change isn't always a bad thing," she said finally.

Lizzie rolled her eyes. "Whatever." They had arrived at the house where Tank the German shepherd lived. "I'll walk Tank and Dottie today if you do Pixie and Pogo."

Maria agreed, and the girls split up to fetch the dogs who were waiting patiently for their walks. Lizzie grumbled to herself as she opened the door and clipped on Tank's leash. Why did Daphne have to stir things up? But as she walked Tank over to Dottie's house, she began to cheer up. It was hard to be too grumbly when you were around dogs, especially dogs as well-behaved as Tank and as sweet as Dottie.

By the time they finished up and said good-bye for the day, Lizzie had forgiven Maria. So they would have an election. No big deal. She knew she could count on getting two votes: hers and Maria's. All she had to do was convince Brianna to vote for her, and Daphne's plan to take over would be history.

Lizzie walked home, feeling like herself again. As she neared her house, she saw a woman coming toward her with a bouncy black dog prancing at her side. Was it a Lab? A poodle? A Labradoodle? Lizzie squinted, trying to make out whether his coat was curly or straight. As she got closer, Lizzie realized that both the woman and the dog looked familiar. "Mom!" she said. "What are you doing with Gus?"

Her mother grinned. "Meet our new foster puppy," she said.

CHAPTER TWO

At the sound of his name, the dog's ears perked up. He shook himself happily until his collar tags jingled, then jumped up onto Lizzie, planting his feet on her chest. "Off!" she cried automatically. Gus was an adorable puppy, with tightly coiled black curls, floppy ears, and a funny face, complete with wiry black eyebrows — but it was never all right for dogs to jump on people, no matter how cute they were.

Lizzie stared down at Gus, then back up at her mother. "New foster? What do you mean?" she asked. Gus was a famous dog: he had been featured a few months earlier in an article in the local paper. In fact, Lizzie's mom, a reporter for the *Littleton News*, had written the article. It had appeared on the front page of the second section, with pictures and everything.

The energetic black Labradoodle — a cross between a Lab and a poodle — had been the ring bearer at one of Littleton's biggest weddings ever. The groom was a policeman named Tommy. The bride, Jackie, was a firefighter like Lizzie's dad. When the article about their wedding appeared in the paper, everybody was talking about it.

Jackie's dog, Gus, had totally stolen the show, prancing up the aisle carrying a red velvet pillow in his mouth. The wedding rings were tied onto it with purple satin ribbons. That turned out to be a lucky thing when Gus decided to play keep-away with the pillow and charged around the church for a full ten minutes. What an uproar! The bridesmaids threw down their bouquets and ran after Gus. The minister tried to tackle him. The mother of the bride chased him up the aisle, and the bride herself chased him back down.

Gus thought it was all just a fantastic game. He ran faster and faster, dodging around the pews. As Lizzie knew, there was nothing a dog liked better than playing keep-away, and the more people to keep something away from, the better. By the time they got the pillow back (an usher finally cornered Gus near the choir stalls), everyone was laughing hard, including the minister. He had to take a break before he could continue the ceremony. Jackie joked that her own dog had gotten more attention than any bride could ever get.

Now, on the sidewalk, Mom laughed. "I surprised you, didn't I?" she asked. "I guess I surprised myself, too. I sure didn't expect to come home with a dog today." She bent to scratch Gus between the ears, and he wriggled all over with happiness and excitement.

Oh, I love the way you scratch me! It makes me want to kiss you!

He leapt up and put his paws on Mom's stomach, reaching his neck up to try to lick her face. Mom giggled. "Gus! Quit it!" she shrieked, but she was laughing.

"Gus, off," said Lizzie. Jumping up was not okay. Didn't Mom know that? When the exuberant puppy ignored her, Lizzie reached out to grab Gus's collar. "Off!" she repeated as she pulled him off her mother. "Good boy," she said when all four of his feet were on the ground. She pulled a treat out of her pocket and gave it to him. "Ow!" she said. "Be gentle." She shook her hand, which he had nipped.

"He didn't mean to hurt you," her mom said. "He's really just a big sweetie. Aren't you, Gussie?" She bent down to scratch his head again.

Lizzie groaned. She knew what was coming next. Sure enough, Gus jumped up. "Uh-uh!" Lizzie said sharply, pulling his collar.

She gave her mom a quizzical look. This was not the way her mother usually behaved around puppies. Not that she was mean — not ever. She was always nice: gentle and sweet and pretty patient. But Mom was not really a dog person. Lizzie knew that in truth her mom preferred cats. "You really like him, don't you?" she asked.

Mom ducked her head and smiled. "I do," she said. "There's just something about this dog. I don't know if it's his funny face or his happy attitude or what, but I think he's irresistible. Maybe that's why I spoke up when I did." She turned toward home and told Lizzie the whole story as they walked. "I went back today to interview Tommy and Jackie. You know, like 'Where Are They Now?' My editor thought it would be fun to follow up, since that first article about the wedding was so popular."

"And?" Lizzie asked.

"They're doing great. Tommy was promoted to sergeant not too long after they got back from their honeymoon. Jackie is thinking she might be ready to have a baby soon." Mom stopped to untangle Gus's leash. "They're very happy in their new home, and they're shopping for a new car. Everything's great — except for one thing."

"Gus?" Lizzie asked. "Is he a problem because he jumps up? I can train him not to do that in no time."

"It's not that," said Mom. "It's Tommy. He's allergic to dogs. Very allergic. He thought he could live with Gus since he's a Labradoodle and doesn't shed much, but ever since he and Jackie moved in together, Tommy is sneezing constantly. His eyes are itchy and his nose never stops running."

"Oh, no," said Lizzie.

"'Oh, no' is right," Mom said. "It's a problem. Jackie loves her pup, but she can't stand to see Tommy feeling terrible all the time. They really tried to make it work, but just this week they decided that they have to give him up. They were going to take him to Caring Paws, but I didn't like to think of this bouncy boy closed up in a kennel like that. So . . . I said we'd take him!"

"Just like that?" Lizzie asked. Caring Paws was a great place — as animal shelters went — but Lizzie knew that it was always much better for puppies to be raised in a family home. Still, she was surprised that her mom had acted so impulsively.

"Just like that." Mom laughed. "Well, I did call

your dad to make sure he agreed. Of course, he was happy to help Jackie out." Lizzie's dad was good friends with Jackie.

Lizzie reached down to pat Gus — gently, so he wouldn't get excited all over again. "Well, I'm sorry for Jackie, but it sure will be fun to have this guy around," she said. "Once we teach him not to jump up, that is. And it shouldn't be too hard to find him a forever family. He's so cute."

"Exactly," said Mom. "Maybe someone will read the article I'm going to write and decide he's just what they are looking for." She pulled a reporter's notebook — the long, narrow type she always carried with her — out of her pocket. "If I get right to work, the story should be in the paper tomorrow."

Lizzie saw Gus's ears perk up when he spotted the notebook. His tail began to wag.

I wonder if that's something to eat!

"Uh-uh, Gus!" Lizzie said before he could jump up to grab the notebook out of Mom's hand. She shook her head at the grinning puppy. "We've got some work to do before you'll be ready for a new home."

CHAPTER THREE

Mom did get right to work. As soon as she and Lizzie got home, she went up to her office. "Bye-bye, Gussie-Gus," she called as she headed up the stairs. "Be a good boy."

Lizzie shook her head as she watched Mom disappear. *Gussie-Gus?* Mom never talked like that to their foster puppies.

Lizzie's younger brothers — Charles and the Bean — were out in the backyard with Dad, playing catch with one of Buddy's toys, a soft, rubbery football that actually flew pretty well. Buddy ran back and forth, following the football's path from person to person.

When Lizzie brought Gus out onto the deck, he stood still for about one millisecond before he took off like an arrow, galloping straight for the toy Charles was about to throw to Dad. Gus's eyes were bright and his ears flew straight out as he rocketed toward Charles, a pink tongue hanging out of his happy, grinning face.

I know this game! I'm great at this game!

"Yow!" said Charles, staggering as Gus practically knocked him over in his haste to grab the toy. "Hey!"

"Gus!" Lizzie yelled. "Bad dog. Bring that here, Gus."

Gus showed no sign that he heard her. He raced around the yard with the football sticking out of his mouth, shaking it wildly as he ran. The squeaker inside the toy squealed crazily as Gus tossed the football into the air and caught it again and again, chomping down with glee each time. Buddy raced after Gus, but he couldn't keep up with the long-legged black puppy, or even get close enough to grab the toy out of the newcomer's jaws.

"Wow, look at Gus go," Dad said admiringly. "He's a real athlete."

"Lizzie, can't you catch him?" yelled Charles. "He's ruining our game."

"Gus! Gus! Gus!" chanted the Bean, clapping his hands and laughing his googly laugh as he watched the dog race by.

"Ignore him," Lizzie said. "He wants to play keep-away, and if we chase him, we'll never get that toy back. We have to just pretend we don't want it and refuse to play the game."

She sat down on the deck, with her back to the yard, and crossed her arms. Dad and Charles joined her, even though they didn't look convinced by her plan. The Bean kept hopping up and down and yelling Gus's name.

"Hush, Beanie," said Lizzie, pulling him onto her lap. "Let's all calm down here, okay?"

Sure enough, once the attention was off him, Gus began to slow down. Soon he ambled to the deck and dropped the football at the bottom of the stairs, then stood back, waiting to see if anyone would come to get it. When Lizzie got up, he grabbed the football again and ran off a few steps. When she sat down, he dropped it and waited, wagging his tail and grinning. "He sure does love to play," Lizzie said, smiling in spite of her frustration. It was hard to be mad at such a cute, goofy, playful dog.

She pulled a treat out of her pocket. "Maybe this will work," she said. She went down into the yard and called Gus, who had run off again with the football. "See what I've got for you!" she said, holding out the treat. The pup trotted over to investigate, sniffed her hand, and let the football fall out of his mouth. "Drop it!" Lizzie matched her command to his behavior, scooping up the football before she handed over the treat. "That's right. Good boy."

"He'll learn quickly." Mom had appeared on the deck. She smiled down at Gus.

"Is the article done already?" Lizzie asked.

Mom shook her head. "I just had to come out to check on Mr. Gus." She smiled bashfully, looking at her feet. "You know, to see how everything was going."

Lizzie raised her eyebrows. Normally, Mom would be thrilled to have some time at her desk without having to look after a puppy.

Dad got dinner going while Mom went back to work and Lizzie and her brothers played with the puppies. When Dad called up the stairs that the food was ready, Mom came down with a bunch of papers in her hand. "It's done," she said. "Just about, anyway. I'll do a little revising after dinner."

Lizzie and Charles fed the puppies. Then everyone sat down to eat. "So what did you say in your article?" Lizzie asked Mom as she passed her a big bowl of spaghetti.

"Want to hear?" Mom picked up the papers and started to read out loud. "'A lot of readers will remember a Labradoodle named Gus and his hilarious antics during Tommy and Jackie's wedding,'" she read. "'What they may not know is that he's the cutest, smartest puppy ever —'"

"Hey!" Charles reached down to cover Buddy's ears. "Don't listen to her, Buddy. Everyone knows that *you're* the cutest, smartest puppy ever."

Mom picked up a pen. "How about '*one of* the cutest, smartest puppies ever'?" she asked. "Will that do?" She read some more, all about how great Gus was (Lizzie noticed that she didn't mention his jumping-up habit), then told the sad tale of how Tommy had discovered his allergies. "'Gus is looking for a new family, and only the finest home will do for this special boy,'" Mom finished.

"Very nice," said Dad. Lizzie noticed an odd tone in his voice. So she wasn't the only one who thought Mom was acting weird. "But isn't the article supposed to be about Tommy and Jackie?"

Mom's cheeks turned pink. "Well . . . I just thought that the dog angle —"

"I'm teasing you," Dad said. "I've never seen you take to a dog this way before. I think it's kind of funny."

"What if someone who reads the article is interested in adopting him?" Lizzie asked. "I mean, maybe the publicity will help us find a good forever home for Gus."

"I'm going to ask my editor if it's okay to put my contact information in the article," Mom said. "Who knows? Maybe the perfect person will read about Gus and e-mail me." She reached down to scratch Gus's head. "Until then, we'll take good care of you," she promised the pup.

CHAPTER FOUR

After breakfast the next morning, Dad took Charles and the Bean with him to run errands. Lizzie was playing with both puppies in the backyard when Mom walked downstairs and out onto the deck. "You're not going to believe what happened," she said. Gus galloped over to Mom and jumped up to say hello, even though he had just seen her five minutes earlier in the kitchen. His tail wagged hard as he put his paws on her belly.

I missed you! Where have you been all this time?

"Gus!" Lizzie said. "Off." She shook her head at Mom. "You have to cross your arms and turn your back on him when he does that," she said, "instead of encouraging him with pats and kisses."

Mom smiled sheepishly. "I can't help it," she said. "He's so cute. And he hardly weighs anything. Somehow I don't really mind when he jumps on me."

"That's not the point," Lizzie said. "He has to learn not to jump up. Other people won't like it. How are we going to find him a home if —"

Mom interrupted her. "Oh, I don't think we're going to have any trouble finding this puppy a home," she said. "Come up to my office. I have to show you something." She led the way upstairs, with Lizzie and both puppies following.

When they got to her office, Mom showed Lizzie the in-box full of e-mails on her screen. "The paper put the story up on their e-edition last night as soon as I turned it in, and I guess it went viral," she said, scrolling down the list. "Lots of people must have posted it and passed it along to their friends. The real paper hasn't even come out yet, but look at all the e-mails I've already gotten!"

Lizzie gaped at the list of subject lines. "'I want Gus!'" she read out loud. "'Gus needs me! Please let me adopt Gus!'" Gus jumped up at the sound of his name. Lizzie petted him as she laughed out loud. "This is crazy," she said. "Where are they all from?"

"I haven't even started to read them," said Mom. "I can see we have our work cut out for us, though."

The phone rang, and Lizzie answered it. "Gus is a superstar!" shouted Aunt Amanda. "I just saw his picture on Facebook!"

"You did?" Lizzie asked. Her head was spinning. "How could that have happened so fast?" There was a beep on the line. "Hold on," Lizzie told her aunt. She pressed a button. "Hello?"

"Hi, I'm calling about that adorable puppy, Gus?" a woman said. "Is he still available?"

"Um . . . what? Wait, how did you get this number?" Lizzie asked.

"I just Googled 'Betsy Peterson, Littleton,'" the woman said. "Please, tell me he's available. I have to have him! He looks exactly like a dog I used to have."

"Can you hold on a sec?" Lizzie said. She switched back to Aunt Amanda. "I have to go," she said. "We'll call you back later. This is nuts."

"Good luck!" said Aunt Amanda.

Lizzie returned to the other caller. "Okay," she said, grabbing a pen and paper from her mom's desk. "What's your name?"

"Hannah Strong," said the woman.

"And where are you calling from?" Lizzie asked.

"I live in Nebraska," she said. "You can ship him to me, right?"

Lizzie's mouth dropped open. "Nebraska? I don't think so."

"But —" the woman began, just as she was interrupted by another beep.

"Hold on," said Lizzie. She punched a button. "Hello?"

The calls kept coming all morning. People phoned from Florida, from California, from Texas, and from Idaho. There was even a call from Sweden! Lizzie took down names and numbers and tried to keep track, but soon her pad was a mess of scribbled notes.

"This is ridiculous," Mom said. She had been reading through the e-mails while Lizzie answered the phone, but now she shut down her computer.

"All these people for one dog? Don't they know there are a million dogs and puppies out there who need homes? Why do they all want Gus?"

At the sound of his name, Gus jumped up and dashed over to Mom for some petting.

"Off, Gus," Lizzie said automatically, almost before he could jump up. "They want him because you made him famous," Lizzie said. "And now we don't even have time to play with him." She threw down her pad and pen. "On top of that, most of these calls were from people I would never give this puppy to, not in a million years." She picked up the pad and looked at her notes. "Like this woman who lives in a tiny apartment. Gus is way too energetic for that. Or these old people. How are they going to keep up with him? Here's a single guy. He sounded nice, but he's super busy with his job. How would Gus get enough attention?" She sighed. "Not to mention that most of these people live way too far away. We're not putting Gus on an airplane."

"It's the same with the e-mails," Mom admitted. "I even got one from a woman who's planning her wedding and wanted Gus to be in it. Just because Gus was in a wedding once, she seems to think a puppy is some sort of accessory, like a pair of shoes or a veil." She scrolled down the list of e-mails. "Or this one, who says she's pretty sure she's not allergic to dogs." She clucked her tongue. "Not to mention that a lot of these people have terrible grammar and punctuation."

"Who cares about that?" Lizzie asked.

"I do," said Mom. "If they're that sloppy in their writing, maybe they just don't care too much about anything. That's not the kind of owner Gus deserves."

Lizzie thought for a second, reaching down to scratch Gus's head. "When the paper comes out, we'll probably hear from even more people who want to adopt him. When have we ever had too many people wanting a dog we were fostering? We'll never have time to interview everyone who wants Gus."

"If only they could interview themselves," Mom said. "We need them to tell us why they deserve our little superstar."

Lizzie was quiet for a moment, thinking. Then she sat up straight. "That's it!" she said. "I've got it!" She almost laughed out loud. She'd always been an idea person, but this was going to be one of her most fantastic ideas ever.

CHAPTER FIVE

"Wait till you hear my great idea! I figured out the perfect way to decide who gets to keep Gus." Lizzie was so excited that her words tumbled over each other.

She had invited Maria, Daphne, and Brianna over to meet Gus, and they had arrived just moments earlier. As each of them came into the house, Lizzie stood with Gus next to her. Before he even tried to jump up, she trapped his leash under her foot, which kept him from leaping too far — a trick she had learned from Aunt Amanda. "Uh-uh," she told Gus when he tried to greet her visitors a little too enthusiastically.

"Gus!" Daphne said. "You celebrity, you." She scratched his ears and let him put a paw up on her belly.

Maria giggled when Gus tried to jump on her. "He's so cute!" she said. "Even cuter than in his pictures."

Brianna stepped away from Gus and turned her back on him, refusing to give him any attention until he calmed down.

"Very nice, Brianna," Lizzie said admiringly. "You know just what to do." She realized too late that she should have reminded each of her friends how to act around a jumping dog — before they came over.

"My family used to have a springer spaniel. Merry liked to jump up, too," said Brianna. "So what's your great idea?"

"An essay contest!" Lizzie blurted out. "It just seemed like the best way to sort through all these people who want Gus." Lizzie led her friends out to the backyard so they could play with Buddy and Gus. "This way, they can tell us about themselves. My mom thought it was a great idea, and her editor already put up a notice about it online." She picked up Buddy's football and tossed it quickly before Gus could jump on her. Both dogs charged after it.

"Who gets to decide which essay is best?" Maria asked. "You?"

Lizzie shook her head. "Our family will read through them all and give the best ones to the judges. Mom and I were thinking the judges could be Ms. Dobbins, my aunt Amanda, and Jackie — you know, Gus's original owner."

Ms. Dobbins was the director of Caring Paws. Lizzie would see her later that day when she went to the animal shelter for her regular volunteer time. "I'm sure Ms. Dobbins will be happy to be a judge," she said. "She's always looking for ways to get more publicity for the shelter. The more people who know about Caring Paws and the work they do, the better."

The puppies came running back, each holding on to one side of the football. Lizzie put out her hand for it and Buddy let go of his side, but Gus did not. He jumped away from her, shaking the toy madly. Then he ran up and down the yard, showing off his prize.

Look what I have! Woo-hoo! Can't catch me!

Maria and the other girls laughed, but Lizzie ignored the prancing pup, knowing that if she reached for the football, Gus would run off with it.

"Are you charging an entry fee for the essay contest?" asked Daphne. "Maybe the contest could be a fund-raiser for Caring Paws."

"Great idea!" said Maria. "And you could announce the winner at the shelter and have a story in the newspaper about it."

"Yeah!" said Brianna. "We could make it a big party and invite everyone who entered. That way, people will come to Caring Paws and see for themselves that there are plenty of other dogs who need homes, not just Gus."

Lizzie stared at her friends. Nobody had even seemed to notice how great *her* idea, about the essay contest, was. All they wanted to do was add their own ideas — which, she had to admit, were actually pretty good. "Wow," she said finally. "Great thinking, everyone. This is going to be so excellent." Gus, realizing that nobody was paying attention, had finally dropped the football. She reached down to ruffle his fur, and without warning he jumped up on her.

Yay! It's about time you gave me some attention!

"Ow! Gus, that hurts. Your toenails are sharp."
Lizzie pushed Gus away.

"It's not his fault," said Brianna. She squatted
down to pick up one of his feet. "Poor Gussie. You
need to have your toenails clipped, don't you?"

Gus leaned against her.

You really understand me, don't you?

"Gus needs an owner like you," Lizzie said.
"Someone with a lot of patience. You're really
great with dogs, Brianna."

Brianna ducked her head. "Gus is special," she
said. "Whoever gets to adopt him is a lucky
person."

"It's not just luck, though," Lizzie said. "The

whole point of the contest is to find the perfect owner for Gus."

"Who do you think that is?" Maria asked. "I mean, what kind of person?"

Lizzie thought for a moment. "Somebody who understands dogs," she said. "Somebody who lives in the country, or who has a yard. Gus wouldn't do well in a city apartment." She stood up. "Hold on," she said. "Let's make a list. I'll go get something to write on." She ran inside and came back with a notebook and a pencil.

The girls brainstormed while they watched Gus and Buddy race around the yard. "Somebody with another dog, maybe?" said Maria. "He loves to play."

Lizzie wrote it down. "He loves kids, too. You should see him with the Bean. He seems to know not to jump up on little ones. He's really gentle and sweet."

"How about an athletic person?" Daphne asked. "Gus would love to hike or run with somebody. And the exercise would help burn off some of his puppy energy."

By the end of their visit, the girls had come up with a long list of things to look for in Gus's new owner. "We'll probably never find someone who has *all* these things," Lizzie said. "But we can try. I can't wait for those essays to start coming in!"

CHAPTER SIX

The essays began to arrive by e-mail the day after the contest was announced. Mom printed a bunch of them out and passed them around after breakfast on Sunday. Lizzie groaned. After the huge stack of Dad's blueberry pancakes she'd eaten, she was more interested in a nap. "Do we have to read them right now?" she asked.

Mom nodded. "Miss Lizzie, this whole thing was your idea," she reminded her. "We're all going to have to pitch in on this or we'll be completely swamped when they start coming in by mail." She handed a stack each to Lizzie, Charles, and Dad. "There are definitely ones that we can put aside right away, like this one." She held up a wad of paper about an inch thick. "Obviously, this person went way over the word count."

The essays were supposed to be 250 words or less, which Mom said was about one typed page with double line spaces.

"What about this one?" Lizzie asked, holding up a sheet of paper with three words typed on it in giant letters: GUS IS ADORABLE! "It's under two hundred fifty words, so the person didn't break the rules."

"But she also didn't tell us why Gus belongs with her and her family," Dad pointed out. "Aren't they supposed to explain why we should choose them as Gus's new owners?"

"Exactly," Mom said. She reached down to pet Gus, who sat near her chair. "Of course he's adorable. Everybody knows that." She made kissy noises at Gus and his ears stood up. "Don't they,

Gussie-Gus?" Gus lunged forward to kiss her, putting both paws up on her lap.

All I know is that you're my new favorite person!

Mom giggled.

"Mom!" Lizzie said. "I keep telling you. You can't let him do that. Stand up and walk away."

Mom obeyed, but she was still giggling.

"He's definitely adorable," Lizzie agreed after she and Dad had rolled their eyes at each other over Mom's behavior. "But aren't all puppies adorable? Well, maybe except for those hairless Chinese crested dogs. Although, if I ever actually met one of those, I'd probably think even they were cute!" She sat for a moment, staring into space, wondering if she had ever seen an un-cute puppy. She couldn't think of a single one.

"Back to work," Mom reminded her. "The contest is over in less than a week."

"Ms. Dobbins is really excited about the party," Lizzie reported. During her volunteer time at the shelter the day before, she had talked to the director of Caring Paws about hosting a party to announce the essay contest winner. Ms. Dobbins had been very enthusiastic, especially when Lizzie suggested that her mom could write an article about the party.

"Look at this one!" Charles said. "I bet it's exactly two hundred fifty words." He started to count. "'I love that cutie Gus.' That's five words. 'I love that cutie Gus.' Another five. 'I love that cutie Gus.' That makes fifteen —"

Mom threw up a hand. "Stop!" she said. "You're right. It's exactly two hundred fifty words. The same words over and over again. I checked it with my computer's word counter. I don't know why I even printed that one out."

"Everybody deserves a chance," Dad said.

They moved into the living room, with essays in hand, and settled in to read. The Bean sat on the floor, playing with Gus and Buddy. He laughed his googly laugh when Gus rolled over onto his back for a belly rub, ears flopping upside down, paws held up in front, a goofy smile on his upside-down face.

The phone rang every ten minutes, it seemed, and they took turns answering it and telling the callers about the essay contest. Lizzie still couldn't believe how many people were interested in Gus. "This is crazy," she said as she leafed through the essays on her lap. "How are we ever going to decide who gets him?"

"We don't decide, the judges do," her mom reminded her. "We just have to find the finalists.

But I'm starting to wonder if I would pass any of these along to the judges. Don't people know how to write? Don't they even know how to use spell-check?" She shook her head, staring down in dismay at an essay she was reading.

"I found a good one," said Charles. "I mean, at least I think it's good."

"Let's hear it," said Dad. "Read it to us."

Charles groaned. "The whole thing?" he asked. He was not fond of reading aloud.

"At least a little of it," urged Mom.

"Okay, here goes," said Charles. "This one is from Farmgirl."

The newspaper had decided that contestants should use pen names instead of their real names so the judging would be fair. They didn't want any personal connections to get in the way.

Charles began to read. "'I would be the perfect owner for Gus. I live on a small farm, where I grow vegetables and raise chickens and goats. There is plenty of room to roam and Gus could spend his days outside with me while I work. I love dogs, even though I have never had one of my own so far. I know I have a lot to learn, but I am a hard worker and I will do what it takes to give Gus a good home.'" Charles paused for a breath.

"She does sound good," said Lizzie. She could picture Gus on a farm.

"I don't know," Mom said. "What about the fact that she's never had a dog before? I think Gus needs an experienced owner." She leaned over to peer at the paper Charles was reading. "Plus, she doesn't know how to use paragraphs and she misspelled 'responsible.'"

"Still," Dad said, "she's got a lot going for her. Let's start a pile for essays to read again and one for entries that we definitely won't pass on to the judges."

Everybody agreed on that plan. By the end of the afternoon, Lizzie's eyes were tired. She was stiff from sitting for hours. And looking at the tiny "read again" pile they had created, she knew they were no closer to finding Gus's perfect owner. This was not going to be so easy.

CHAPTER SEVEN

"Please pass the Special Chicken," said Lizzie.

"*My* Special Chicken!" said the Bean, waving his fork around so bits of Special Chicken flew through the air.

"Uh-uh," Mom told the Bean as she passed the container to Lizzie. "It's your favorite, but remember? We all share."

Dad had brought home takeout from China Star, a reward for all the work everyone had been doing on the essay contest. Lizzie figured that by dinnertime on Wednesday night, she had read over thirty essays. It was amazing how many people loved and wanted Gus.

Or maybe it wasn't so surprising. Gus was pretty special. After a few days of having him around, Lizzie was almost as in love with Gus as Mom was. He was so cute, and so smart, and such a happy, sweet boy. Now she smiled down at him and rested her hand on his head. "You're a good boy," she told him. "You're not even begging. Pretty unusual for a dog who's part Lab."

Gus gazed up at her and thumped his tail.

If I'm such a good boy, how about a bite of that chicken?

"He really is a good boy," Mom agreed. "He's not even jumping up as much."

Lizzie had finally convinced her mother that she had to discourage Gus from jumping. As soon as Mom had started crossing her arms and turning her back on him, Gus had learned quickly that jumping up was not a good way to get attention. Almost magically, he had stopped doing it — at least, most of the time. Sometimes when he was extra excited, he just couldn't help himself.

Lizzie took a few bites of the dish her family called Special Chicken (General Tso's Chicken on the menu), followed by a forkful of beef with broccoli, the dish Dad always ordered. She had already eaten her spring roll, her favorite, and watched enviously as everyone else ate theirs. She liked her family's system of sharing, but she dreamed of someday having a whole order of spring rolls all to herself. Would she order her usual, shrimp? Or maybe go for something different and order pork? Lizzie considered the question as she ate some of Mom's favorite: delicious, slurpy, noodle-y veggie lo mein.

"Are you ready, Lizzie?"

Lizzie realized she had not been paying attention to the conversation. "Ready?" she asked.

"Have you picked out your favorite essay to share with us?" Mom asked.

Each night, the family had gathered to read their favorite essays out loud and vote on which ones to pass on to the judges. So far they had a pile of about ten that everyone really liked. Well, not everyone. Mom had not been crazy about any of them. She always found something wrong. The people who lived near a lake seemed nice, but they were about to have a baby, and Mom worried that Gus wouldn't get enough attention. Lizzie thought the woman who was a dog trainer sounded amazing, but Mom didn't like her grammar and punctuation. And as for Dad's favorite so far, the guy who wanted to train Gus as a Frisbee-catching dog, Mom thought he was just too young to take on the responsibility.

"I do have a favorite," Lizzie said. "Ready to hear it?" She wiped her mouth and took her empty plate to the sink. Then she picked up her pile of essays from the counter and leafed through it to find the one she liked. "This is from a girl about my age," she said. "She and her family sound great. Her pen name is Iheartdogs." She began to read. "'I think we would be the perfect family for Gus because we all love dogs. We have been wanting a new dog ever since our last one died, and we have a lot of love to give. I have one younger sister and we live with our parents in a big old house with a huge yard. I know a lot about dogs and I am even a partner in a dog-walking business.'" Lizzie looked up. "Just like me!" she said. "How cool is that?"

She went on reading, becoming more and more convinced that this person sounded like a great owner for Gus. When she finished, she passed the essay to Mom. "What do you think?" she said. "She even spelled everything right, as far as I can tell."

Mom glanced at the essay. "Not bad," she admitted. "But it sounds like both parents have full-time jobs away from home. Gus would be alone while the kids are at school."

Lizzie rolled her eyes. "Mom," she said. "That's not unusual. Plenty of dogs spend time alone every day. Maybe it's not perfect, but as long as they are comfortable and safe and have fresh water and all that, it's fine. Think how happy he'd be when they all got home every day!"

Mom seemed unconvinced. She didn't like the essay Charles had chosen, either, by a young woman who was an artist. "That's not a very stable profession," she said. "What if she runs out of money and can't take proper care of Gus?" And she didn't like the one Dad had picked out. "A family with six kids? Are you kidding? Gus would get lost in the mix."

"What about your favorite?" Lizzie asked her mom. "Did you find one you liked?"

"Sure!" Mom held up a crayoned drawing of a black dog in a field of grass with a rainbow arcing overhead. "I know it doesn't meet the requirements of the contest," she said. "But isn't it cute? It really looks like Gus."

Lizzie sighed and pushed away from the table. She was tired of the whole contest and wished she had never come up with the idea. It was a good thing that it would all be over by Friday night.

"Tell you what," Mom said. "I know this has been hard. How about if we go out for a creemee as a special treat?"

"Yay!" yelled the Bean. "Creemees!"

Lizzie and Charles gave each other a high five as they raced out to the van. They loved going to the soft-serve ice cream stand. They each had their favorites there. Charles always got the Dish of Dirt: vanilla ice cream with hot fudge, crushed Oreos, and gummy worms. Lizzie's choice was a waffle cone with a vanilla-chocolate twist and rainbow sprinkles. Even the dogs would get a treat: a small amount of vanilla ice cream in a bowl, with a dog biscuit on top.

Lizzie had delivered the dog treats to Gus and Buddy, waiting in the van, and was just enjoying the first delicious lick of her cone when she spotted Maria and her parents getting out of their car. "Hey!" she called, waving. It was always fun to run into friends at the creemee stand.

But Maria didn't wave back. Instead, she frowned at Lizzie as she took her place in line.

Lizzie gulped. She knew that face. It wasn't the first time her best friend had been mad at her. But what had she done now?

CHAPTER EIGHT

"What did I do?" Lizzie cornered her friend as soon as Maria had picked up her ice cream: a small butterscotch sundae, the same thing she always ordered.

"You know," Maria said without looking at her. She sat on the bench of a picnic table and dug into her treat.

"I don't!" Lizzie said. "Come on, why are you mad?" She licked her cone, trying to control the drips, which were coming faster and faster.

Maria frowned. "I'm just tired of the way you're kissing up to Brianna these days. You're all, 'Oh, Brianna, you're so good with dogs!' and 'Wow,

Brianna, I like your new sneakers.' You don't miss a chance to compliment her. You make sure she gets to walk all the most fun dogs, and I noticed you gave her one of your cookies at lunch the other day." It all spilled out in one big rush. Then Maria crossed her arms and glared at Lizzie.

"But —"

"But nothing. You know I'm right. And I know what you're up to. You're just trying to get her to vote for you as president." Maria stabbed her spoon into her ice cream and took a huge bite.

Lizzie gulped. Suddenly she felt like she had a rainbow sprinkle stuck in her throat. She gave a little cough. "I just —"

"You just want everything your way, all the time," Maria said. "That's what."

Lizzie's ice cream was melting fast. Now there were chocolate and vanilla streams running down over her hand. She'd only taken one napkin, and it wasn't enough to mop up the stickiness. "Wait a sec," she said. She ran to the trash can and dumped her cone. She only wished she could have given the melted mess to Buddy and Gus, but she knew that chocolate was bad for dogs. She ran back to Maria. "I'm sorry," she said. "You're right."

Maria gaped at her. "What?"

Lizzie shrugged. "You're right. I didn't even completely realize I was doing it, but I guess I was. I do want Brianna to vote for me. I want to keep being president. Is that really such a crime?"

Her friend looked surprised. "Well, no. I guess not. But why don't you just see how the voting goes? You agreed that it was fair to have an election." Maria pushed her dish toward Lizzie. She could never finish a whole sundae, and Lizzie usually helped her out.

"True," said Lizzie, taking a bite and letting

the sweet butterscotch roll around on her tongue for a moment. "But only because you all ganged up on me."

"We did not gang —" Maria was starting to sound mad again.

"I know, I know," Lizzie said. "It's the democratic process, right? May the best woman win." She polished off the last bite of ice cream and grinned at Maria. "I just hope everybody agrees that I'm the best woman."

By Thursday, the contest deadline, the entries had dwindled to a trickle. "I guess the timing was about right," Mom said as the family gathered in the living room after dinner that night for one last session. Once again they'd each brought their favorites, and once again Mom had provided a treat: this time it was hermit cookies from the bakery downtown.

Lizzie bit into the soft brown bar. "Yum," she said. She loved the spicy, raisin-filled cookies.

"Yum," Charles echoed.

"Yum, yum, *yum!*" the Bean shouted, rubbing his tummy. "Hermans are my favorites."

"Hermits," Lizzie said, correcting him.

The Bean nodded. "Hermans," he said, taking another joyful bite.

"So," Dad said. "Any favorites today? I've got a couple."

"So do I," said Lizzie. She was particularly happy with one of them, from a woman who said she'd had three Labradoodles already and loved the breed — even though they could be "a little overly enthusiastic." It was good that she knew what she was getting into.

"I have one," said Charles. "A guy who teaches people how to butcher meat. I bet he'd have a lot of good leftovers for Gus. You'd like that, wouldn't you?" he asked the black pup, who lay next to him with his head on Charles's lap.

Gus rolled over onto his back for a tummy rub, waving all four feet in the air.

Oh, goody. It's about time I got a little attention.

"Awww!" said Mom as they all cracked up. "Gussie-Gus loves those tummy rubs, doesn't he?"

Gus seemed to fit in so well with their family, Lizzie thought. He loved everyone, and everyone loved him. He and Buddy had a blast playing together, and Gus was learning every day. He hardly ever jumped up anymore, though he often wriggled all over with the effort it took to keep all four feet on the ground.

"I have a favorite tonight, too," said Mom. She waved a paper.

Everybody turned to stare at her. "You?" Lizzie

asked. "You actually found an essay that you thought was good enough?"

Mom shrugged. "Well, maybe. At least the spelling is good — grammar, too. I liked the way this person described her family. It sounds like a very loving home."

"Read it," Lizzie said.

Mom looked down at the paper. "It's from FosterMom," she said. "Listen to how she starts. 'Gus would be the perfect addition to our family. We have three younger children, all of whom love and understand dogs and puppies. We have one dog, a sweet little guy who always gets along well with other dogs. How do I know this? Well, because we have been a foster family for quite some time, and have taken care of many puppies who needed homes.'"

"Hold on," said Dad. "This family sounds awfully familiar."

"I know!" said Mom. "Isn't it funny? Maybe that's why I like them so much."

"But if they already have one dog and they foster other puppies, could they really handle Gus, too?" Lizzie asked. "Or would they have to give up fostering puppies?"

Mom shrugged. "They'll have to figure that out," she said. "They sound like responsible people, so I'm sure they would do the right thing." She went on reading the essay, and when she was done, she put it on the "yes" pile without even asking.

Lizzie looked at her mom, wondering just how much she had fallen in love with Gus. Enough to secretly enter a contest?

CHAPTER NINE

Lizzie woke up on Friday with a smile on her face. It was the day of the big party at Caring Paws. Then she remembered something, and her smile faded. It was also the day she would have to say good-bye to Gus. The contest judges would spend all day reading the essays her family had selected. Then, at the party, they would reveal their choice — and Gus would go home with that person.

"Gussie!" she said, reaching down to pet behind his ears, where his coat was especially soft and springy. He jumped up from where he lay sleeping on the rag rug, and put both paws up on the bed. "Okay, you can come up," she said, patting the blanket beside her. He leapt up and snuggled in next to her, rolling over for a tummy rub and stretching his legs as he sighed with pleasure.

I could stay here forever.

"You know we'd keep you if we could," Lizzie told him as she stroked his soft belly. "But you know and I know that there's no way we would still be able to foster puppies if we had two of our own." She scratched his ears next, wondering if *Mom* knew. Lizzie was not ready to give up fostering, even if it meant they could keep this adorable puppy.

She lay there as long as she could, but then Mom called up the stairs that it was time for breakfast. After that there would be school, and then dog walking, and then a rush over to Caring

Paws to decorate the party room and get ready for the big event.

Oh. Suddenly she remembered that there was something else to dread about today. She hated to even think it, but could this be her last day as president of AAA Dynamic Dog Walkers? They had decided to hold their weekly meeting and have the big vote at Caring Paws, after they had decorated but before the party. Lizzie felt her stomach tighten into a knot when she thought about that. Would Brianna vote for her? Would — she gulped — Maria?

Lizzie pulled Gus toward her for one more snuggle, then hopped out of bed and pulled on her favorite jeans and tee.

"Have a fun time with Gus," she told her mom as she headed out the door for school. "Enjoy your last hours together." When she saw her mother's face fall, she knew that Mom was as sad as she was about saying good-bye to Gus. Lizzie turned and threw her arms around her mom, giving her a big, long hug. She hugged Gus, too, then headed out the door. It was time to face the day.

Why was it that the school day could drag on forever and ever if you knew you had something special and fun to do afterward, but fly by in a flash if you were dreading something — for example, an election? School let out before Lizzie knew it, and her dog-walking time went by in a blink. It seemed like only minutes had passed since she'd gotten out of bed, but now here she was in the party room at Caring Paws with Maria, Daphne, and Brianna. They'd come to decorate for the party — and to have their meeting, too. Lizzie's stomach was tight with a special blend of excitement and worry.

"Is there any more of that purple crepe paper?"

she asked Maria, who was holding one end of a long yellow streamer while Lizzie pinned the other to the wall.

"I don't think so," said Maria. "But I don't think we need it. In fact, I think we're just about done." She looked around the room, nodding to herself.

Streamers hung gaily from one side to the other, over the rows of chairs. Brianna and Daphne had set a long table with tablecloths, paper plates, and paper cups — all in an adorable puppy-paw-print design. The girls had also set up a little stage for the announcement of the contest winner, and piled dog biscuits into bowls for people to give the pups they visited during the special shelter hours after the presentation.

Lizzie and her friends had made sure that all the dogs up for adoption looked spiffy and that their cages were extra clean. It wasn't often that you had a whole roomful of people who were ready to adopt a dog. They had to make the most of the occasion.

"Done?" Lizzie asked. "You think? I don't know. Shouldn't we make signs or something?" She knew she was stalling. As soon as the room was decorated, it would be time for their meeting. She was really not looking forward to this voting business.

Maria shook her head. "It's time. The party's starting soon. Let's get the meeting going." They sat down at the table, and Maria passed out pens and pieces of scrap paper. "We might as well vote right away and get that over with," she said.

"Wait a second. How can this be a secret vote?" Brianna asked. "We all know each other's handwriting. Whoever reads the papers will know who we voted for."

"We'll ask Ms. Dobbins to look at them," Lizzie said. "She can keep a secret. She and the other judges have been reading those essays all day and she hasn't let a single clue slip about which ones they like best."

Brianna nodded.

"That sounds fair," Daphne agreed.

"Fine with me," said Maria.

"Let's vote, then," said Lizzie. She took a deep breath and let it out slowly. She looked around the room at the others, who were busy writing on their papers. Maria's shiny black hair hung down, helping to hide what she was writing.

For a moment, Lizzie wondered wildly if she should vote for Maria. Maria was the best! She was smart, and organized, and kind, and she had great ideas. Why shouldn't she get to be president? Lizzie closed her eyes for a second. Then she opened them and leaned over her paper. Using her arm to hide what she wrote from the others, she printed her own name: *L-I-Z-Z-I-E*.

Everyone folded their papers and put them into an "I HEART DOGS" mug Lizzie had found on a shelf. "I'll go get Ms. Dobbins," she said.

A few minutes later, Lizzie held her breath, feeling her heart beating wildly inside her chest as Ms. Dobbins pulled out the first scrap of paper and began to unfold it. She seemed to take forever to do it, but finally she read the name: "'Lizzie.'"

Lizzie let out her breath with a whoosh, then sucked it back in when she heard the next vote.

"'Maria.'"

Lizzie gasped when Ms. Dobbins opened the third paper and read the name on it. "'Brianna.'"

And she groaned when the director read the last one. "'Daphne.'"

"You have got to be kidding me," she said. "I

don't believe it." Without really thinking about it, she reached out and took the papers from Ms. Dobbins's hand. "Let me see those," she said.

The other three girls jumped out of their seats and started to yell, but it was too late. Lizzie had already figured out what had happened.

CHAPTER TEN

"This is ridiculous," Lizzie said, crumpling all four papers in her fist. "You all voted for yourselves."

"And so did you, obviously," Daphne added right away. "So what? I think I'd make a great president. I guess we all think we would."

Ms. Dobbins burst out laughing.

"It's not funny," Lizzie said. "Now what do we do?" She noticed that Maria was giggling, too. Then Brianna snorted back a laugh, and even Daphne started to smile.

"It *is* kind of funny," said Ms. Dobbins. "But here's what I'd say. From what I've seen, you're all amazing young women with lots to offer. You're all smart and good leaders, and you care very much about animals. Why not forget about having a president and just be four equal partners in your business?"

For a second, the room was silent. Then Maria spoke up. "Great idea. I like it," she said.

"Me too," said Brianna.

"I'm in," said Daphne, nodding.

Lizzie took a deep breath. Then she let it go, along with her wish to be president for life. What else could she do? Ms. Dobbins was 100 percent right. In a way, it was a relief to have the whole thing over with. Being president was a big responsibility. Why not share it? "Sounds good," she said with a grin. "Now, isn't it time for the party to get started?"

As soon as Ms. Dobbins opened the shelter doors, people began to flood in. Soon the party room echoed with excited talk and laughter. Lizzie spotted Mom and the rest of her family arriving, and waved to them. Brianna's mom and little sister arrived soon after, and Daphne's parents, and Maria's mom and dad.

The judges — Ms. Dobbins, Lizzie's aunt Amanda, and Jackie — stood near the podium set up on the little stage, having one last whispered conversation. Then Ms. Dobbins walked to the podium and asked everyone to settle down.

"Where's Gus?" a guy yelled from the back of the room. "We want Gus!"

Ms. Dobbins smiled and held up her hands. "Of course you want Gus. That's why we're all here, isn't it? He's here, back in one of the kennels. We didn't want him to get overwhelmed." She looked around the room. "There are a lot of people here, for one dog," she said. "This is a new experience for me, and for the shelter." She paused and smiled.

"Before we announce our essay contest winner, I just want to say that we have twelve dogs and seven puppies back there with Gus, any one of whom would make a terrific addition to your family. We hope you'll take some time to get to know them after this program — and if anyone is inspired to adopt, we will be thrilled to help you out. I'm offering a reduced adoption fee tonight, and some of our generous sponsors have added donations, like a month's worth of free dog food, a free vet checkup, and a free training session."

Lizzie whooped and began to applaud, and the crowd joined in. Ms. Dobbins shot Lizzie a grateful smile before she leaned into the microphone again. "I want to say that being a judge for this contest was one of the most heartwarming experiences I've ever had. I really enjoyed reading your essays and hearing about all the love you have to offer a rescued pet."

Jackie stepped forward. "If I can just add something," she said, "it was a wonderful experience for me, too. I want the best home possible for my sweet Gus, and there's no question that any of you would offer him a special place."

Now Lizzie's aunt stepped up. "But we did have to pick a winner," she said. "It wasn't easy. In fact, it was next to impossible. We ended up with two essays that we thought were the most convincing, and since we couldn't end the contest in a tie, we basically flipped a coin."

"And our winner," said Ms. Dobbins as a hush came over the room, "is the writer known as FosterMom."

Applause rang out. Lizzie looked around the room to find the winner. For a moment, nobody stood up. Then Lizzie watched in shock as her very own mother got to her feet. "Mom!" she burst out.

Mom bit her lip and held up both hands in a "what can I say?" gesture. Then she walked to the front of the room. Ms. Dobbins, Jackie, and Aunt Amanda looked almost as shocked as Lizzie felt.

Mom bent her head to speak into the microphone. "Thank you to the judges," she said. "I'm glad they liked my essay. But . . . I can't accept the prize. I can't accept Gus. For those of you who don't know, I am Betsy Peterson, the writer who wrote the article about Gus, and the mom of the family who has been fostering him. I — well, I guess I sort of fell in love with him, just the way all of you did. And for a while I convinced myself that he belonged with our family." She looked at the ground. "But we are a foster family. We take care of puppies like Gus who need homes, and we need to be able to continue doing that.

They need us, those puppies, and if we took Gus, we really wouldn't have space in our home for them." She looked out at Lizzie and gave her a smile. Lizzie nodded and smiled back. She was proud of her mom.

Ms. Dobbins sniffed and wiped away a tear. "Phew," she said. She laughed a little. "Thank you, Betsy. The puppies do need you, and so do I."

Jackie gave Mom a hug. Then she faced the microphone. "I guess that means that our other favorite is the new winner," she said. "Is Iheartdogs here?"

Lizzie smiled. That was the essay she had chosen. She looked around the room again and grinned when she saw who stood up. It was Brianna!

Brianna clapped her hands and shrieked. "Really? We get to keep Gus? Forever and ever?"

She threw her arms around her mom, and then the whole family trooped up to the stage.

"Congratulations," Ms. Dobbins said, handing Brianna a red leash. "I know that Gus could not have found a better home."

Brianna thanked her and turned to Jackie. "You can come visit him anytime," she said. "Or take him for a walk. I know he'll always be happy to see you."

Jackie threw her arms around Brianna. "Thank you," she said. "I know you'll take good care of my boy."

Ms. Dobbins stepped to the microphone. "And thanks to all of our contestants," she said. "I hope you'll come meet our shelter dogs. Who knows? Maybe a new member of your family is waiting just beyond these doors."

As the room emptied, Lizzie found her mom and

gave her a long hug. Then she ran to catch up to Brianna. "So it was you," she said. "You did a great job on your essay. It was my favorite."

Brianna smiled and ducked her head. "Thanks. Sorry your family didn't get to keep Gus."

"That's okay," said Lizzie. "It's more important to me to keep fostering. And anyway, I'll get to see him all the time, since he belongs to one of the equal partners in our business!" She grinned at her friend and held up her hand for a high five.

As they walked through the doors to the kennels together, eager to see Gus and the other dogs, Lizzie stopped to take a deep sniff. She loved the smell of dogs and the sounds of their happy barks as they greeted all the new people who walked up and down the aisles. *Pick me!* she imagined them saying. *Me! Me! Me! Take me home!* She smiled as she watched people checking out the available dogs and puppies. She had a feeling that Gus would not be the only one going home with a new family that night. And who knew? Maybe she could convince Mom to let her foster one — or two! — of the puppies.

PUPPY TIPS

Sometimes when people decide to adopt a dog, they have a type in mind. Maybe they are looking for a dog just like one they used to have or they are hoping to find a particular breed. When you're ready to adopt, it's great to have an idea of what kind of dog will be best for your family — but it's also good to be open to meeting a dog you didn't expect to love. You might go to the animal shelter looking for a superstar puppy like Gus and go home instead with a tiny terrier or an older dog who needs the special kind of love you can give him. Take your time and keep your heart open, and you will find the right dog for you and your family.

Dear Reader,

This book came out of the idea that it would be interesting for the Petersons to foster a puppy everybody wanted. It was fun to figure out how and why that would happen. By the time I finished writing about Gus, I almost wanted a sweet, energetic Labradoodle myself! But like the Petersons, I already have my hands full. As much as my dog, Zipper, would like a buddy, I think one pooch is enough for now.

Yours from the Puppy Place,
Ellen Miles

P.S. If you liked reading about a Labradoodle, you'll love NOODLE, about a golden doodle. And for another famous dog everybody loves, try MUTTLEY.

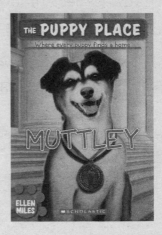

THE PUPPY PLACE

DON'T MISS THE NEXT PUPPY PLACE ADVENTURE!

Here's a peek at

LOLLIPOP, SNICKERS, AND PEANUT!

"We're almost there!" Maria said. "I can smell the piney woods." She stuck her nose out the car window and sniffed.

"Just a little longer," her mom agreed, from the front seat. "Good thing, too. I bet Simba is about ready for a walk."

Lizzie turned in her seat to check on Simba, the big yellow Lab riding in the way back. "Is that true, Simba?" she asked, giving him a scratch between the ears. Simba gave her a doggy grin and panted happily. As a guide dog (he belonged to Maria's mom, who was blind), he was not supposed to get petted while he was working. That meant he especially loved attention when he was "off duty." A long car ride definitely counted as off duty.

Lizzie Peterson loved going to the Santiagos' weekend home in the woods, even if it did take forever to get there. She loved the forest, the trails, and the sparkling lake. Most of all, she loved the cozy cabin, and the sweet tiny room she shared with Maria, her best friend. The only thing she didn't like was that she had to leave her darling puppy, Buddy, behind.

"You'll have Simba to spend time with," Mom had said when Lizzie begged to take Buddy along. "And the rest of us would miss Buddy if he went away."

It was true. All the Petersons loved Buddy, the foster puppy who had come to stay. Lizzie's family took care of puppies who needed homes, usually just until they found each one the perfect forever family. She and her two younger brothers, Charles and the Bean, always had a hard time saying good-bye to the puppies they had helped care for. In Buddy's case, saying good-bye had been impossible. When it was time to find him a home, the whole family agreed that he belonged right there with them.

Lizzie closed her eyes, picturing Buddy's smooth brown coat and the heart-shaped white patch on his chest. He loved it when she scratched him there. She hoped Charles would remember to do that while she was gone. She sighed. Buddy would be fine. It was only a few days, after all. Meanwhile, she and Maria would be having a fantastic time at the cabin. With luck, the lake would still be warm enough for swimming, and she and Maria planned to hike and climb trees and build fairy houses out of moss and sticks and bark. Even though the cabin was in the middle of the woods, there was always plenty to do.

Lizzie's stomach rumbled. She was ready for a snack, especially since she knew that even once they arrived they would still have to hike in to the cabin, pulling wagons loaded with all their stuff. She reached into the backpack at her feet and rummaged around until she found the candy bar she'd brought. "Want some?" she asked Maria, as she peeled back the crinkly paper.

Maria's eyes widened. She held up her hands and shook her head. "Oh," she said. "I guess I forgot to tell you."

Mrs. Santiago swiveled around to face them. "Do I smell chocolate?" she asked.

"No, Mom," Maria answered quickly. "It's just —

nothing." She made a motion to Lizzie, pointing to the backpack. "Put it away," she mouthed.

"Why? What's going on?" Lizzie asked.

"Didn't you tell her?" Maria's mother asked.

"I meant to," said Maria. "But —"

Mrs. Santiago shook her head. "Lizzie, we've agreed that this is going to be a sugar-free weekend. Our family has been getting into the sweets a little too much lately, and we all decided we needed a break."

ABOUT THE AUTHOR

Ellen Miles loves dogs, which is why she has a great time writing the Puppy Place books. And guess what? She loves cats, too! (In fact, her very first pet was a beautiful tortoiseshell cat named Jenny.) That's why she came up with the Kitty Corner series. Ellen lives in Vermont and loves to be outdoors every day, walking, biking, skiing, or swimming, depending on the season. She also loves to read, cook, explore her beautiful state, play with dogs, and hang out with friends and family.

Visit Ellen at www.ellenmiles.net.